To
Nolan.
Happy reading
trails.

Georgia Graham

A Team
Like No Other

Red Deer Press

Dad whistled and Stephen threw open the gate.
One, two, three, four dogs shot out. Then Dad
helped five, six, and seven into their boxes
on the back of the truck.

"Come on, Skoki," called Dad.
"We can't have a team with only
seven dogs. We need eight."

But the big dog paused at the gate until Stephen wrapped his arms around her neck and snuggled his cheek into her. "You're the best dog ever," he whispered into Skoki's plush fur. Then away she darted into her box.

Dad closed the door on the dog boxes and opened a smaller door in the center of each one. The huskies poked out their grinning faces.

Dad drove until great jagged mountains towered all around. Stephen wished he was riding in the dog box with Skoki, the Chinook wind in their faces.

Dad steered the heavy load up the last stretch of winding icy road. When the truck stopped, the huskies yelped with excitement.

Dad unloaded the sled and anchored it to the truck. He attached each dog's harness to the main cable until all eight huskies were howling and lunging forward.

Stephen grabbed the bucket of dog treats and jumped into the sled. Once Dad set his feet on the back runners, Stephen looked up and nodded.

Dad released the anchor.

"Mush," shouted Stephen — and they were off.

Skoki and Timber were in front, plowing a new trail through the heavy snow.
"Run, Skoki!" Stephen called out. "Go, Timber!"
His voice echoed off the mountains and danced up and down the valley.

"Haw!" Dad shouted.

Skoki and Timber led the team left onto a trail. When Dad hollered, "Gee!" the dogs turned right out onto a wide frozen lake. The team carved giant zigzags into the clean, flat surface.

"Is it time for the dogs to have a treat?" Stephen called back.

"Sure," laughed Dad. "Whoa," he boomed as he pressed his foot onto the brake between the runners.

The team came to a halt. The dogs rolled face first in the snow. Stephen handed out biscuits and pats on the head.

Skoki wagged her tail and gently took the biscuit in her teeth. When the dogs had gulped down every last crumb from the snow, they were ready to go again.

"Which trail should we take?" asked Dad.

"I like the trail where we can look over the cliff," said Stephen, tumbling into the sled.

"We can see if the eagle nest is still there," said Dad.
"Mush!" they both shouted, and off they raced to the most wonderful trail of all.

Suddenly the sled hit something hard, slamming Stephen flat on his back.
He struggled to his knees and turned to Dad.

But Dad was far behind, fighting his way onto his feet in waist-deep snow.

"Whoa!" he called, but his words were swallowed up in the wind. Stephen could hear the call, "Whoa, whoa!" as it grew fainter and fainter.

Without Dad's weight on the runners, the team travelled rapidly over the bumpy trail, and Stephen was thrown from side to side. He held on tight.

"Stop, dogs!" he cried. But the dogs barrelled ahead, unheeding.

"Stop, stop!" Stephen yelled. Now that he could see the cliff ahead he turned cold with fear. He breathed a prayer and with all his strength shouted, "WHOA, Skoki!"

Skoki threw herself to the ground at the very edge.

Thump! Whump! Crunch!

Seven dogs smashed into Skoki. The sled skidded onto the top of the pile of huskies.

There was a sudden silence.

Stunned, Stephen peered out of the sled.

Dad struggled up to them, one boot off, his face dripping in sweat, gasping for air. He yanked the sled back to safety, then wrapped Stephen in the biggest hug ever.

Meanwhile the dogs untangled themselves and stood up, whining. All but one. Skoki lay motionless.

Dad ran his hands over Skoki, feeling her carefully.

"When will she get up?" cried Stephen. Dad didn't answer.

Stephen threw his arms around Skoki's neck.

"Come on, Skoki. We need you. You're the best dog ever."

The husky's tail twitched. Then it started moving, in big sweeps. Slowly Skoki stood up and took two limping steps. Dad ran his hands over her again.

"I don't think anything's broken," he said.

Skoki rode back to the truck in the sled with Stephen, who gave her hugs and pats all the way.

Skoki, Timber and the other dogs were a team of eight. But a boy and his dog — that's a team like no other.

Published in Canada by Red Deer Press, 195 Allstate Parkway, Markham, ON, L3R 4T8
www.reddeerpress.com

Published in the U.S. by Red Deer Press, 311 Washington Street, Brighton, Massachusetts 02135

Edited for the Press by Peter Carver
Cover and text design by Blair Kerrigan/Glyphics
Printed and bound in China by Sheck Wah Tong Printing Press Ltd.

We acknowledge with thanks the Canada Council for the Arts, and the Ontario Arts Council for their support of our publishing program. We acknowledge the financial support of the Government of Canada through the Canada Book Fund (CBF) for our publishing activities.

Library and Archives Canada Cataloguing in Publication
Graham, Georgia, 1959–
A team like no other / written and illustrated by Georgia Graham.

ISBN 978-0-88995-360-4

1. Dogsledding—Juvenile fiction. I. Title. II Series.
PS8563.R33T42   2004   jC813'.54   C2004-901592-3

To my models:
  My nephew, Jairus Pow (Stephen)
  My brother, Brian Pow (Dad)
  Brian's dog team (the huskies)
Also, thank you to my family, the Pows, for their totally different versions of what happened the day of the wild ride.
Especially Stephen and Jody Pow who were in the sled.

– Georgia Graham